What Does It Mean to Be Green?

Eco-Pig Explains Living Green

By Lisa S. French

Illustrations by Barry Gott

magic
wagon

Eco-Pig

visit us at www.abdopublishing.com

For Agnes—LSF

Published by Magic Wagon, a division of the ABDO Group, 8000 West 78th Street, Edina, Minnesota 55439.

Looking Glass Library™ is a trademark and logo of Magic Wagon.

Printed in the United States.

 Manufactured with paper containing at least 10% post-consumer waste

Text by Lisa S. French
Illustrations by Barry Gott
Edited by Stephanie Hedlund and Rochelle Baltzer
Interior layout and design by Nicole Brecke
Cover design by Nicole Brecke

Library of Congress Cataloging-in-Publication Data
French, Lisa S.
 What does it mean to be green? : Eco-Pig explains living green / by Lisa S. French ; illustrated by Barry Gott.
     p. cm. – (Eco-Pig)
 Summary: In rhyming text, Eco-Pig explains how simple it is for everyone to "live green."
 ISBN 978-1-60270-665-1
 [1. Stories in rhyme. 2. Pigs–Fiction. 3. Environmental protection–Fiction. 4. Green movement–Fiction.] I. Gott, Barry, ill. II. Title.
 PZ8.3.F9085Wh 2009
 [E]–dc22
                        2008055336

Dear friends of the earth,
I just have to insist
that you pay close attention
to this tale with a twist.

It belongs to a pig
who hangs out in a tree.
His name is Bernard,
but we call him E.P.

The *E* stands for eco,

short for ecology.

That means he cares for our planet.

Listen up, and you'll see.

5

One moonlit fall night
in a town called To-Be,
strange noises were heard
in a green apple tree.

6

What was making that noise?
Now, what could it be,
that snorting and snuffling
in the green apple tree?

7

By the light of the moon
the To-Bes gathered about,
when through the shivering leaves
out poked a pig's snout.

8

"Good golly, gracious, there's a pig in our tree! Why has he come?" asked Grandpa To-Be.

"I have come," said E.P.,
"because my snout led me here!
Once I sniffed your clean air,
there was nothing to fear.

"Then I sniffed your fresh flowers,
your mountains, your streams,
your forests, and your pastures.
It's the town of my dreams!

11

"But something is wrong here,
in this grand eco scene.
When I start to sneeze,
that means someone's not Green!"

Tiny To-Be looked at her hands,
her feet, and her knees.
"We do come in all colors,
more than just green, if you please."

"When you are Green," said E.P.,
"that just means that you care,
for Earth, this great planet,
our home that we share.

14

"If we live a little less large
and a little more lean,
we'll help keep our home cool
and we'll help keep it clean."

15

"Being Green sounds too hard!"
sighed Teen To-Be.
"It's quite easy," said Lou,
"and you can learn from E.P."

"First, please get me a tissue
and a nice cup of tea.
My snout has an issue
with Mr. Watts of To-Be.

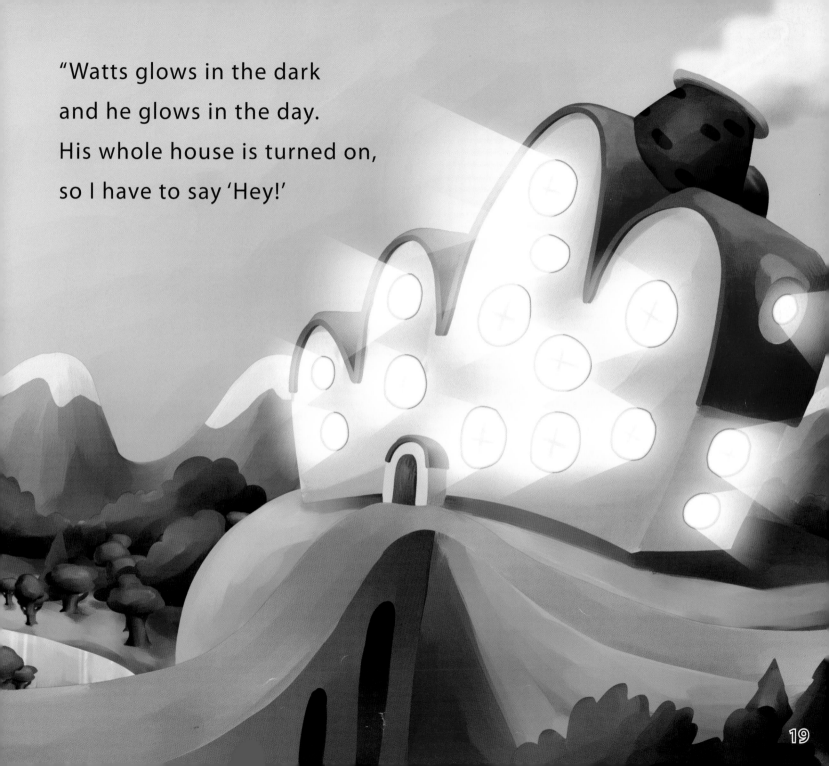

"Watts glows in the dark
and he glows in the day.
His whole house is turned on,
so I have to say 'Hey!'

19

"When we plug in too much
we burn too much fuel,
which pollutes planet Earth.
Now we know that's not cool!

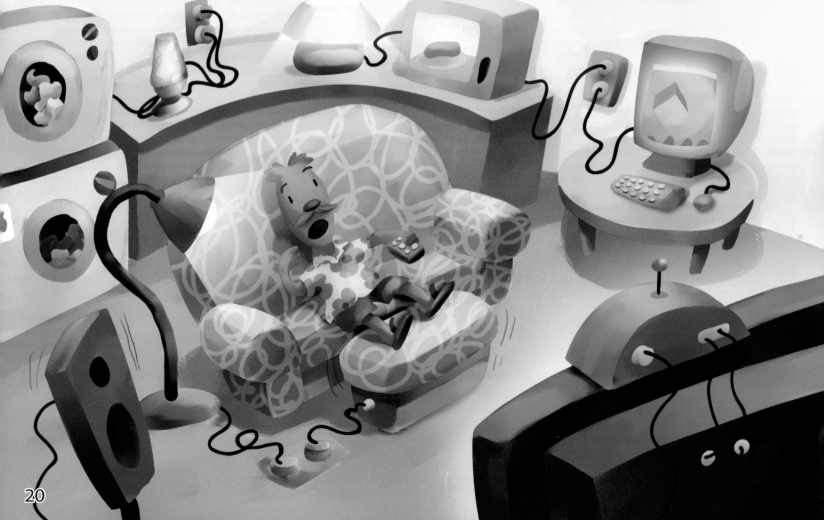

"So turn it off and unplug it.
Don't use more than you need.
Just use your fair share.
That's the way to succeed!"

21

But just at that moment
the Guzzlers drove by,
trailing exhaust fumes.
Oh my goodness, oh my!

They drove round and round,
and E.P. started to wheeze.
Whoa! Let's step on the brakes
and get them bicycles please.

You can ride bikes to the store,
to the park, and to school.
So let's ride and breathe easy.
It's an Eco-Pig rule!

They all grinned as they rode
to see the Heaps of To-Be.
There, they learned that recycling
is fun, easy, and free!

The Heaps recycle it all,
old clothes and old shoes,
cans, plastic, and glass,
and yesterday's news.

Recycle the rainwater.

Don't let it go down the drain.

Water your grass and your garden.

Wash your sheepdog Duane.

"If you live Green," said E.P.,
"you can be sure of one thing:
our planet will thank you.
You will hear her heart sing,

in the wind and the stars,
the bluebirds and the bees,
in you and in me,
and the green apple trees!"

Words to Know

ecology—a branch of science that studies the connection between plants and animals and their environment.

exhaust—the gas and fumes that come from an engine.

Green—related to or being protective of the environment.

pollute—to make the environment unclean with man-made waste.

recycle—to break down waste, glass, or cans so they can be used again.

Green Facts

- Recycling one ton of paper, saves: 17 trees, 6,953 gallons of water, 463 gallons of oil, 587 pounds of air pollution, 3 cubic yards of landfill space, and 4,077 kilowatt-hours of energy!

- The average American uses 650 pounds of paper every year. We could save 100 million tons of wood each year if all that paper was actually recycled!

- Americans go through 2.5 million plastic bottles every hour.

- Recycled plastic is made into many things, including plastic lumber, clothing, flower pots, insulation for sleeping bags and ski jackets, and car bumpers.

- Recycling one aluminum can saves enough electricity to run a television for three hours.

- Last year 39 million appliances were recycled. The steel from those appliances would have been enough to build about 160 football stadiums.

More Ways to Green-i-fy!

Talk to your mom and dad about
what you can try at home:

1. Turn down your heat by just five degrees.
2. Switch off lights you don't need.
3. Use fans instead of air conditioners to cool down the house.
4. Take showers rather than baths.
5. Use energy-saving lightbulbs.
6. Wash dishes by hand instead of using the dishwasher.
7. Avoid using disposable products, such as paper napkins.
8. Don't leave water running when brushing your teeth and washing your hands.
9. Check for leaks in faucets.
10. Plant a vegetable garden.